W9-CHY-485

Very Short Mother Goose Tales to Read Together

by

MARY ANN HOBERMAN

Illustrated by

MICHAEL EMBERLEY

Megan Tingley Books

LITTLE, BROWN AND COMPANY

New York   Boston

*For Mother Goose and all
the children who love her.*
—M.A.H.

*To the Big Cheese. For all the trust,
support and patience.*
—M.E.

Text copyright © 2005 by Mary Ann Hoberman
Illustrations copyright © 2005 by Michael Emberley

All rights reserved. In accordance with the U.S. Copyright Act of 1976, the scanning, uploading, and electronic sharing of
any part of this book without the permission of the publisher is unlawful piracy and theft of the author's intellectual property.
If you would like to use material from the book (other than for review purposes), prior written permission must be obtained
by contacting the publisher at permissions@hbgusa.com. Thank you for your support of the author's rights.

Little, Brown and Company

Hachette Book Group
237 Park Avenue, New York, NY 10017
Visit our website at www.lb-kids.com

Little, Brown and Company is a division of Hachette Book Group, Inc.
The Little, Brown name and logo are trademarks of Hachette Book Group, Inc.

The publisher is not responsible for websites (or their content) that are not owned by the publisher.

First Paperback Edition: September 2012
First published in hardcover in July 2005 by Little, Brown and Company

Library of Congress Cataloging-in-Publication Data

Hoberman, Mary Ann.
    You read to me, I'll read to you : very short Mother Goose Tales to read together /
by Mary Ann Hoberman ; illustrated by Michael Emberley. — 1st ed.
    p. cm.
    ISBN 978-0-316-14431-5 (hc) / ISBN 978-0-316-20715-7 (pb)
    1. Nursery rhymes — Adaptations. 2. Children's poetry, American. 3. Nursery rhymes, American. I. Emberley, Michael. II. Title.
PS3558.O3367Y67 2004
811'.54 — dc22   2004007569

10 9 8 7 6 5 4 3 2

SC

Printed in China

The illustrations for this book were done in pencil, watercolor, and dry pastel on 90-lb. hot-press watercolor paper.
The text and display type is set in Shannon.

Table Of Contents

Author's Note:

Here is another read-together/read-aloud book, the third in the You Read to Me, I'll Read to You series. This time nursery rhymes provide the point of departure. As in the other books the text itself indicates who reads what when. And like the previous book, which playfully revised some of our most familiar fairy tales, this one takes similar liberties with many of our best-loved nursery rhymes.

This book is for readers of all stages and ages: pairs of beginning readers, young or old or young *and* old, as well as pairs made up of a beginner and a more-advanced reader. The book also lends itself to choral readings; in many of the schools I have visited, groups of children, sometimes half the class, read each part. And of course readers can always switch parts and colors and read the stories again, so that they get a chance to play all the characters!

While most children are probably familiar with the nursery rhymes reworked in these pages, I recommend that parents and teachers initially recite the original versions with their new readers to add to the fun.

And once again I acknowledge the admirable work of ProLiteracy, whose dedicated tutors continue to offer the gift of reading to students young and old.

Introduction

Here's another book,
Book three –

I'll read to you!

You'll read to me!

It's different from
The other times:

This time we're reading
Nursery rhymes!

But while we'll recognize
Each name,
The things they do
Are not the same.

They're not the verses
That we knew
When we were only
One or two.

We'll read each page
To one another.

You'll read one side,
I the other.

The middle words
Like these before us
We'll read together
In a chorus.
So now we know
Just what to do:

You'll read to me!

I'll read to you!

5

Humpty Dumpty

I'm all cracked up.
I really hurt.
And look! I tore
My pants and shirt.

I must admit
I don't know whether
I can put you
Back together.

The King's men tried;
His horses, too.
But there was nothing
They could do.

Well, I'm a doctor
As you see;
But eggs are not
My specialty.

Dear Doctor Brown,
Please take a try.
If you don't operate,
I'll die!

Dear Humpty Dumpty,
Don't despair!
I'll do my best
On your repair.

Why, Doctor Brown,
You've done so well!
You've patched me up!
You've fixed my shell!

Dear Humpty Dumpty,
That's so kind —
And now my fee
If you don't mind.

Why, Doctor Brown,
You charge a fee?
My operation
Wasn't free?

I never heard of
Such a thing!
Why don't you ask
Your friend the king?

I'll have to tell him
What you charge.
I hope your bill
Is not too large.

I've never fixed
An egg before.
I'll have to charge
A little more.

How much is that?

A dollar five.

Why, that's a lot!

Well, you're alive!

Why, yes, I am!

Then pay my fee.
If you're alive,
It's thanks to me!

Humpty Dumpty
Sat on a wall.
Humpty Dumpty
Had a great fall.
The doctor came running;
He got there at ten
And put Humpty Dumpty
Together again!

Jack, Be Nimble

I will not jump, Jane!

        Jack, why not?

That candlestick
Might be quite hot.

        But Jack, the candle
        Is not lit.

I still will not
Jump over it.

        It isn't even
        Very high
        But you won't jump it.
        Tell me why?

I'll jump a wall,
I'll jump a box,
Across a stream
Or over rocks.
But since it is
A silly trick,
I will not jump
A candlestick.

        Just take one jump.
        I wish you would.
        A single jump,
        I think you should.

If you're so sure
What I should do,
Go jump yourself!
I dare you to!

        The candlestick
        Might be quite hot.

It isn't lit.
Have you forgot?

I think it looks
A little high.

It's very short.
Now will you try?

All right, I will.
I'll jump it now.
But only if
You show me how.

It isn't hard
As you can see.
Just start to run
And follow me.

Oh, Jack, you jumped it!
You were good!
You jumped so high!
I knew you could!

You tricked me, Jane!
I should have known.
But now go do it
On your own.

Well, here I go.
I'll start way back.
I'll run! I'll jump!
I made it, Jack!

Jack, be nimble!
Jane, be quick!
They both jumped over
The candlestick!

9

Jack and Jill

My name is Jack.

My name is Jill.

We both were climbing
Up the hill.

The hill was steep

And very high

But at our house
Our well ran dry.

We climbed and climbed
Along the trail

To fetch some water
In a pail.

We didn't have
A lot of time.

We'd gotten tired
From the climb.

And when we finally
Reached the well
And filled our pail,

Guess what? I fell!

Everybody knows our story.
It is really very gory.

I must have tripped
And I fell down.
I scraped my knees
And broke my crown.

I tumbled after
Down the hill.

The townsfolk cried,
"Poor Jack and Jill!"

We both were hurt.
We went to bed.

My mother bandaged
Up my head.

It really was
A scary sight

But pretty soon
I felt all right.

So once again
We climbed the hill
And each one took
A pail to fill;
And after we
Had reached the well,
Neither of us
Tripped or fell.
We filled our pails
Up to the top.
(We didn't lose
A single drop.)
This time the water
Didn't spill,
And that's the tale
Of Jack and Jill!

11

Jack Sprat

I'm Mister Sprat.

> I'm Mrs. Sprat.
> My husband's thin.

My wife is fat.

> I like to eat.

And I do, too,

> But I eat different things
> Than you.

You like your beef
On buttered bread.

> You nibble lettuce leaves
> Instead.
> I eat sausage,
> Eggs and ham.

I eat toast
Without the jam.

> Jack, dear, will you
> Pass the cheese?

Pass the carrots,
If you please.

> No matter what we're served, it's fine,
> Since he eats his and I eat mine!

Pork or lamb chop,
We can share it.

Here's the fat, dear.
I can spare it.

> Here's the lean, dear,
> And the bone.

Here's the ice cream.

        Here's the cone.

And every time
We eat our dinner

        I get fatter.

I get thinner.

        You get thinner.
        I get fatter.

You get rounder.
I get flatter.

        Our doctor says
        I'd better stop
        Or pretty soon
        He fears I'll pop!

Our doctor says
It's very clear
That pretty soon
I'll disappear!

        Our doctor's put us
        On a diet.
        We've both agreed
        That we will try it.

        Jack Sprat, he now eats fat.
        His wife, she eats some lean.
        And still between
        The two of them
        They lick the platter clean!

Little Jack Horner and Little Tommy Tucker

I'm Little Jack Horner

          And I'm Tommy Tucker.

I sit in a corner.

          I sing for my supper.

You sing for your supper?
Why, what do you sing?

          Whatever I want to,
          Just any old thing.

You sing and they feed you?
Is that what you do?

          Yes, white bread and butter.
          Now what about you?

I don't have to sing
For my supper, not I!
I don't do a thing
For my yummy plum pie.

          Why, Jack, I have never
          Had pie in my life!

I'd cut you a piece
But I haven't a knife.

I don't have one either
To cut up my bread.
Do you have a fork
I might eat with instead?

I don't have a fork;
But if you'd like a plum,
Why not do as I do
And stick in your thumb?

Don't you get scolded
For eating that way?
If somebody notices,
What do you say?

If somebody notices
When they come by,
I laugh and I say,
"What a good boy am I!"

But you are the messiest
Fellow I've seen!

I'll lick off my thumb
And I'll get it all clean.

Little Jack Horner
Sat in a corner
Sharing his Christmas pie.
Tom Tucker then said,
"Taste a bit of my bread."
And Jack Horner said he would try.

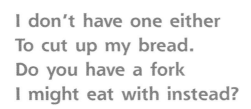

Little Boy Blue and Little Bo Peep

I'm Little Boy Blue.

I'm Little Bo Peep.

We've problems with
Our cows and sheep.

I fell asleep
Beneath the hay
And while I slept
They ran away.

My sheep are lost.
They can't be found.
They disappeared
Without a sound.

My cows went, too.
They're in the corn.
I think I'd better
Blow my horn.

Sometimes if mine
Are left alone,
They wander back here
On their own.

I'll blow my horn,
I'll blow it now.

Oh, look, I think
I see a cow!

I think I see
Some sheep as well.

I think they're mine!

How can you tell?

Their tails are wagging.
That's the sign
That lets me know
These sheep are mine.

Well, here are mine.
They're coming, too.

How do you know
They're yours, Boy Blue?

They're full of burrs
From head to toe.
It's from the meadow
Where they go.

Now that they have
Come back, Boy Blue,
What is the next thing
You will do?

The haystack's here.
I'll nap a bit.

I'll nap here, too,
Right under it.

Little Boy Blue
And Little Bo Peep
Are under the haystack
Fast asleep.

Little Bo Peep
And Little Boy Blue
Have each found their sheep
And they're all asleep, too!

Little Miss Muffet

I'm Little Miss Muffet.
I'm here on my tuffet.

> And I am a spider
> Now hanging beside her.
> Pray, what is a tuffet,
> Dear Little Miss Muffet?

A tuffet's a mound
Where I sit on the ground.

> And what do you eat
> When you sit on your seat?

Why, I eat curds and whey.
They're my breakfast today.

> I do not know those words.
> What is whey? What are curds?

They are made from milk.

> How?

You must go ask the cow.

> May I sit on your tuffet
> Beside you, Miss Muffet,
> And take a short rest?
> I will be on my best.

If my tuffet were wider,
You might, Mrs. Spider;
But as you can see,
It will seat only me.

'Though I see it is narrow,
I'm slim as an arrow.
Oh, please let me sit!
I am sure I will fit.

I have to confess
There's no thing I like less
Than a spider. I pray,
Will you please go away?

I don't understand
Why each time that I land
At the end of my thread,
I fill people with dread.
I am nice and polite
And I don't often bite.

Well, in that case, please stay.
We shall share curds and whey.

I may sit on your tuffet
Beside you, Miss Muffet?

Yes, sit with me here,
Mrs. Spider, my dear,
And we'll have a fine time
While reciting this rhyme:

Little Miss Muffet
Sat on a tuffet
Eating her curds and whey.
Along came a spider
And sat down beside her
And rested the rest of the day!

Old King Cole and the Cat and the Fiddle

I'm Old King Cole.
I'm a merry old soul.

        I'm Hey Diddle Diddle
        The cat with a fiddle.

A fiddling cat! That's very rare.
I've never seen one anywhere!

        Well, that's because there's never been
        A cat who plays a violin,
        Not even one except for me.
        I was a kitten prodigy.

Well, we'll soon see if you're the best
For we shall put you to the test.
My fiddlers three are here today
And they'll decide how well you play.

        I'll tune my fiddle up right now
        And after that I'll show you how.

Well, hurry up! No time to waste.
I hope your tune is to my taste.

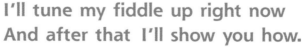

I'll start to play. Please listen, King.

Why, cat, that is a lovely thing!
My fiddlers three all like it, too.
They'd like to learn that tune from you.

I'll give them lessons if you wish.

What do you charge?

A tuna fish.

I'll send my fishermen to sea
To catch a tuna fish for me.

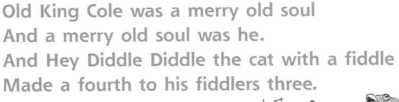

Why, thanks a million, Old King Cole.
You really are a nice old soul.

You splendid cat, please play some more.
My fiddlers three shall now be four.

Old King Cole was a merry old soul
And a merry old soul was he.
And Hey Diddle Diddle the cat with a fiddle
Made a fourth to his fiddlers three.

Old Mother Hubbard

I am Mother Hubbard's dog

      And I am Mother Hubbard.

She's looking for a bone for me.

      I'm looking in my cupboard.

      The cupboard's bare. There's nothing there.
      There's nothing there to eat.

I wish that it were full of bones

      And also bread and meat.

Perhaps we could put on our boots
And walk down to the store
And ask the butcher for a bone
And maybe something more.

      Why, that's a very good idea!
      He knows you love a bone;
      But since it's very cold outside,
      Let's call him on the phone.

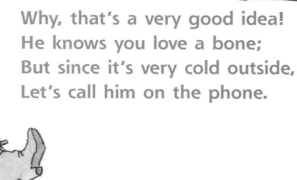

Bow wow! Is this the butcher shop?
Is Mister Butcher there?
This is Old Mother Hubbard's dog.
Have you a bone to spare?

And while you've got him on the phone,
Please ask if he is able
To spare a bit of meat as well
To put upon our table.

Hurrah! Hurray! The butcher says
He has some meat to give her!
He also has a loaf of bread
And what's more, he'll deliver!

Oh, look, here comes the butcher boy;
He got here in a minute!
Let's light the fire in the stove
And roast our dinner in it

And warm my paws

And toast my bread

And after that
We'll go to bed.

Old Mother Hubbard
Went to her cupboard
To fetch her poor doggy a bone.
The cupboard was bare
But they didn't care;
The doggy just picked up the phone!

Peter, Peter, Pumpkin Eater

I am Peter.

I'm his wife.

I've liked pumpkins
All my life.

Pumpkins cooked
And pumpkins raw,

They were all
I ever saw.

Pumpkins raw
And pumpkins cooked,

Pumpkins
Everywhere I looked.

Pumpkins night
And pumpkins day,

So one day
I ran away.
I was worried
That you'd find me.
Then I heard you
Close behind me.
In an instant
I was caught!

Then I had
A clever thought!
I picked you up
I gave a yell
And put you in
A pumpkin shell!

I started in
To cry and shout:
Peter! Peter!
Let me out!

Only if
I hear you say
You will never
Run away.

Only if
I hear you swear
No more pumpkins
Anywhere.

No more pumpkins?
Are you sure?

No more pumpkins.
That's the cure.
No more pumpkins.
Do you swear it?

Yes, although
I cannot bear it.

Don't be sad,
Dear husband, Peter.
You can be
An orange eater.

Oranges are
Orange, too,
Just like pumpkins;
That is true.

Peter, Peter
Pumpkin Eater
Had a wife
And got to keep her,
Gave up pumpkins
For his wife
And they stayed happy
All their life!

Pussycat, Pussycat, Where Have You Been?

Who am I? The pussycat.

    And who am I? The queen.

I called on you in London
And guess what we have seen?

    A little mouse,
    A tiny mouse,

    It gave me quite a scare.
    I shouted, "Eek!" I could not speak
    And jumped up on a chair!

I said, "Be calm, Your Majesty,
You need not be afraid."

    I said, "If you can trap that mouse,
    You will be nicely paid."

The mouse said, "Please, Your Majesty,
This comes as a surprise
For I am just a little mouse
And you're ten times my size."

    "Why, yes, I am," I did reply,
    "Yet you are fully grown!"
    And so I climbed down from the chair
    And sat upon my throne.

I said, "It's not a good idea.
To let that mouse go free.
I'll capture it and eat it up
For you, Your Majesty."

The mouse cried, "Eek!" It gave a squeak
And jumped up on my arm.
"Please save me from that cat, dear Queen!
Please keep me safe from harm!"

I gave a purr and looked at her.
She was a tiny beast,
While I was large and rather plump,
Five times her size at least.

"Let's all be friends," I said to cat.
"Come here and sit with me.
Some cream for you, some cheese for mouse,
And I shall have some tea."

And so we sat upon the throne,
The mouse, the cat, the queen.
The cat and queen sat side by side.
The mouse squeezed in between.

Pussycat, Pussycat,
Where have you been?
I've been to London
To visit the queen.
Pussycat, Pussycat,
What did you there?
I made two new friends.
They're a wonderful pair!

Simple Simon

I am Simple Simon.

And I, I am a pie man.

We both are going to the fair.
We'll walk together till we're there.

Do you have cherry pie today?

I did not hear. What did you say?

I asked if you had cherry pie?

No, none today for you to buy.

Well, if not cherry, how about peach
And apple? I'll take one of each.

Apple pie? I just ran out.
Nor have I any peach about.

A lemon pie, do you suppose?

A lemon pie? I've none of those.

Perhaps a berry pie for sale?

My berry pies are very stale.

I'd like to try one anyway.

I threw them all out yesterday.

Mr. Pie Man, will you tell me:
Have you any pies to sell me?

Well, to tell the truth, dear Simon,
I am really not a pie man.

Not a pie man!

No, not I.
I have never baked a pie.

Never baked a pie? Not one?

Not a pie, a cake, or bun.

Then why are you dressed up like that
In pie man suit and pie man hat?

I'm on my way to baking class
To learn to bake. I hope I pass.

You don't know how to bake?
That's funny!

Simon, have you any money?

Not a penny, it is true.

That is pretty funny, too,
Trying to buy pies today
Without a penny you could pay!

I admit it wasn't wise
But I was hungry for some pies.

Then come with me to school, please do,
And learn to be a pie man, too;
For if you bake your pies yourself,
You'll always have some on your shelf.

Simple Simon met a pie man
Going to the fair.
Said Simple Simon to the pie man,
"Let me taste your ware."
Said the pie man to Simple Simon,
"Show me first your penny."
Said Simple Simon to the pie man,
"Sir, I haven't any."
Said the pie man to Simple Simon,
"My wagon, too, is bare.
Let's both go off to baking school
And learn pie-making there!"

29

Baa Baa Black Sheep

Baa Baa Black Sheep
Have you any wool?

> Now that's a silly thing to ask!
> You know I've three bags full!

That's quite a lot of wool to have.
I'm sure it makes you hot.

> I'm hot until my coat is sheared
> And after that I'm not.

But after they have sheared your wool,
You must feel very bare.

> Oh, soon it will grow in again
> So, really, I don't care.

I'd like to buy a bag of wool
To make a coat for me.

> I'm sorry, sir, but you cannot.
> It's not for sale, you see.

What, not for sale? That isn't fair.
Why, that is why I came.

> One bag is for my master, sir.
> Another's for my dame.

But that adds up to only two.
A third bag does remain.

That bag is for the little girl
Who lives down in the lane.

Well, if I can't buy wool from you,
I'll have to find another.

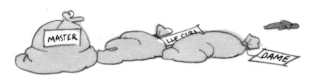

That won't be difficult, kind sir.
We'll go and find my brother.

Is he a black sheep just like you?

No, sir, his coat is white.

And does he have three bags of wool?

I don't know, but he just might.

Baa Baa White Sheep
Have you any wool?
Yes, sir, yes, sir
Three bags full.
One is for the rooster
And one is for the goat
And one is saved for you, sir,
To weave a fine new coat.

The End

It's over.

    Over.

Done.

    All done.

    We really had
    A lot of fun.

Those folks from Mother Goose
Are great.

    The things they did.

The things they ate.

    And there are many
    Other rhymes,
    Lots of rhymes
    From olden times.

    The Queen of Hearts
    Who Made Some Tarts—
    We can arrange it
    Into parts!

There Was an Old Woman
Who Lived in a Shoe—
We can divide it
Into two!

    Let's find some more
    And when we do,
    You'll read to me!
    I'll read to you!